# TAKEN BY THE MOUNTAIN MAN

## WILD HEART MOUNTAIN: MILITARY HEROES
### BOOK TWO

### SADIE KING

LET'S BE BESTIES!

A few times a month I send out an email with new releases, special deals and sneak peeks of what I'm working on. If you want to get on the list I'd love to meet you!

When you join you'll get access to all my bonus content which includes a couple of free short and steamy romances plus bonus scenes for selected books.

Sign up here:
authorsadieking.com/bonus-scenes

# TAKEN BY THE MOUNTAIN MAN

## WILD HEART MOUNTAIN: MILITARY HEROES BOOK TWO

**She's alone in the woods, mine to take, mine to protect...**

When I discover the frightened woman camping on her own with a storm coming, my protective instincts kick in.

There's an evacuee center in town, but there's no way I'm taking Leonie anywhere but my mountain cabin.

Something's got her spooked, and I'll stand guard all night if that's what makes her feel safe.

But when the new day dawns, there's no way I'm giving Leonie up.

This curvy beauty is mine.

*Taken by the Mountain Man* is a forced proximity, age gap, instalove romance featuring an ex-military mountain man and the curvy, innocent woman he takes as his own.

Copyright © 2023 by Sadie King.

All rights reserved.

No part of this book may be reproduced in any form or by any electronic or mechanical means, including information storage and retrieval systems, without written permission from the author, except for the use of brief quotations in a book review.

Cover designed by Cormer Covers.

This is a work of fiction. Any resemblance to actual events, companies, locales or persons living or dead, are entirely coincidental.

Please respect the author's hard work and do the right thing.

www.authorsadieking.com

1

# SYMON

Dark clouds heavy with rain hang on the horizon as I drive the last section of Black Saddle Road. Up here is the highest elevated campground on the mountain, and I need to make sure there are no stray tourists defying the weather warning.

There was a steady stream of hikers descending the mountain today and stopping in at the Ranger lodge to let us know they were off the mountain. Experienced hikers won't stay around with a heavy storm brewing and a severe weather warning. But there are always a few who are too stupid, or too stubborn, to evacuate.

This is the last stop. Then I can get myself home before the storm hits knowing that everyone on my mountain is safe.

My pickup pulls into the campground as thunder rumbles up the valley, making my windows shake. The thick clouds have enclosed the evening in almost total darkness as I park my pickup in the vehicle bay.

This is the most remote and most basic camping spot on Wild Heart Mountain. It's a small clearing with no room for a lot of cars. It's for hikers doing one of the trails that pass over the ridge and across the border into Tennessee.

Not a popular trip at this time of year, so I'm surprised when my headlights skim over a tent. It's tucked into the corner under a large pine tree at the edge of the site. A thin two-man tent that's positioned into the wind and right under the biggest tree in the clearing.

It's not where I'd want to sleep with a storm coming. Whoever put that tent up knows nothing about camping. There's no car either, which means they're both ignorant and stubborn. The worst kind. They've probably been planning the hike for months and refuse to give it up because they won't let a once in a decade storm ruin their plans.

I get out of my truck as the wind blasts icy cold, making my jacket rattle around my collar. It whistles thorough the trees, shaking the branches and sending leaves scattering to the ground.

Anyone camping in this weather must be insane, and the rain hasn't even started yet.

I trudge toward the tent, gearing myself up to placate an angry tourist. I'll have to drive them back down to Hope, the small town on the side of the mountain, and deposit them at the hotel. There'll be complaints about the cost of accommodations and cutting their plans short.

People think being a Mountain Ranger is all about looking after the mountain, but it's as much a people facing job as anything. I've been told I've got a certain charm, and I guess I like people more than some of my ex-military buddies on the mountain, because I generally don't mind dealing with tourists.

After I came back from the military, I joined the guys from my unit here on Wild Heart Mountain. It's a beautiful place and as good as any to start fresh. Which is what I needed.

My military buddies all moved as deep into the mountain as they could to lick their wounds. I understand that. I came back the least damaged of us all. But even I didn't want to live in the town. I've got a ranger cabin at the base of the mountain, and that suits me just fine.

There are two towns here. Hope is the biggest and where all the tourists flock to in high season. Then there's Wild. Which is a little more, well, wild.

It's smaller and less visited by tourists, especially since a motorcycle club took up residence. I served with the president of the Wild Riders MC and they're decent guys, but it's hard to shake the image of the badass motorcycle club.

I reach the small tent and clear my throat, giving whoever's inside plenty of warning that I'm here. The best way I've found in a situation like this is to put on a charm offensive. Be the friendly ranger looking out for their safety. Which is exactly what I am.

"Hello, this is Symon. I'm a ranger here on Wild Heart Mountain."

A blast of wind carries my voice away, and I try again.

"I'm the park ranger. There's a storm coming, and we're evacuating the camping sites on the mountain."

The tent flaps in the wind like it's about to take off, but there are no movement from anyone inside.

"Hello," I call again.

I wait for a few moments, but there's still no response.

"Is anyone here?" I glance around the clearing, looking for signs of life. Maybe they're out hunting their dinner or something, which will be pretty hard in this wind. Even the animals know to hunker down when there's a storm brewing.

I'm about to lift the flap and look inside when a woman comes flying out of the tent. She's wielding a small stick, held up like a weapon, and her face is contorted into a scream.

2

# LEONIE

There's a bear circling my tent. The scuffling noises and growly sounds can only be a bear. But with the wind making such a racket in the trees, I can't be sure. My fingers are numb from cold, but I still pick up the only weapon I can find, which is the nail file I keep in the side pocket of my purse. I don't know what good that will do against a bear, but it makes me feel more confident to be armed.

The beat of my heart is thundering in my ears, almost drowning out the wind. The wind whips around the tent, making the flaps billow in and out. I should have zipped it up when Grant left, but I thought he was only popping out for a pee. That was two hours ago.

Two hours that I've been waiting in this tent as

the sky got darker and darker. I crept out to find him after a while, thinking he might have gotten lost. His suped up Subaru that we drove up in was gone. I stood there for a full twenty minutes; my mind unable to grasp the truth that my gut already knew. Grant had abandoned me.

He abandoned me on the side of a mountain with what looks like the storm from hell rolling up the valley. And to think I was planning on giving him my v-card tonight. He's been pestering me to go all the way since we started dating a few weeks ago. I should have known that when a sports loving guy like Grant shows interest in the chubby girl, it's got to be a practical joke.

Stupid me for falling for it. Now I'm stuck here for the night where there's no cell reception and a storm coming in.

The wind is making such odd noises as it tears through the trees that it sounds like a human voice. I strain my ears to listen. There it is again, a human wail catching on the wind.

My heart almost falters. What if there are not only bears on this mountain but ghosts too? The thought sends a shiver down my spine.

I have no idea why I agreed to come up here for the night. It sounded romantic, camping on the side of a mountain. But now all I want is to be home in

Charlotte. In my city apartment where you can't feel the wind because the other tall buildings block it out and the heating banishes the cold. And where every night I have every single light in the house on to banish the darkness that is fast setting in.

Because yeah, I made the mistake of opening up to Grant and telling him I'm scared of the dark.

*Stupid.*

I should have known when he asked me what my biggest fear was that he was planning something. But I was too struck by the fact that a guy like Grant was interested in me to pick up the warning signs.

So he's never read a book in his life and his idea of a good time is seeing how many beers he can drink before falling over. I ignored the niggling feeling in my gut about him, because he paid attention to me.

If his friends smirked when he introduced me, I pretended not to care. If the other girls in their circle looked at me with pity, I thought it was because I was overweight and younger than them.

But now it all makes sense. I was a dare. Date the fat girl and play a practical joke on her. Find out her biggest fear and drop her right in it.

Because getting stranded in the dark with only my cellphone for light is the worst imaginable situation he could have dropped me into.

My fingers grip my nail file, and a new determination courses through my veins. It might be a bear out there or a ghost, but whatever is out there circling my tent will not take me down without a fight.

With my heart racing and a newfound courage, I rush out of the tent with a war cry on my lips and run smack into a solid wall.

At least that's what it feels like. A wall of muscle. My head tilts back and my gaze travels up and up until I land on the rugged face of the biggest man I've ever seen.

His chiseled jaw pulls into a smile that dances in his pine green eyes. My mouth pops open in shock, and the battle cry dies on my tongue.

"You alone in there?"

His words jolt me back to reality. It's not bears or ghosts I have to worry about. It's strange men in the night who might do bad things to me.

"I've got a weapon."

I brandish the nail file as I take a step back from him, needing to put distance between my thundering heart and the wall of muscle.

An amused look creeps into his eyes.

"What are you going to do with that?"

My hand trembles as I glance at the file. I can barely see it in the dark, and the realization that night is closing in sends a wave of panic through me. The darkness presses on my chest, making my breath short and my pulse race.

Bad things happen in the dark, and this stranger is proof.

I dart away from the man and behind the large pine tree by the tent. There's an opening into the woods, and I run down the narrow trail.

"Hey, where are you going?"

The man starts after me, spurring me on further into the woods. The foliage is thick above me, blocking out the last of the light, and I cry out as I'm engulfed in total blackness.

"Hey, I'm not going to hurt you…"

The man's speaking to me, but I can't make out what he's saying over the wind. I need to get away but the darkness restricts my chest, making it hard to breathe. My legs are like jelly and I sink to the forest floor, trying to push down the panic that's rising in my body as the pressure in my chest gets unbearable.

My eyes squeeze shut, blocking out the dark, blocking out the shadows and the memories that overwhelm my mind. I press my hands to my skull, trying to still my brain, but the memories are too much. I'm gasping for air as the panic attack over-whelms me, tossing me about on waves of terror.

Suddenly, strong arms wrap around me and I'm lifted to my feet. One arm goes under my thighs, the other around my back as he pulls me to his chest. A strong chest that's warm and solid, and I lean into it.

"Hush, little one. I've got you."

The voice is soft and unfamiliar, but it's kind and comforting and gives me a thread of light to cling on to.

I dare to open my eyes. I'm pressed against the muscular chest of the mountain man. My cheek presses against his khaki shirt, the steady beat of his heart easing the panic and stilling my pulse. *Wild Heart Mountain Ranger* is emblazoned on his breast pocket.

As he carries me out of the woods, my mind calms. I breathe in his pine scent and bury my head in his chest as he takes me away from the darkness.

3

SYMON

*T*he woman trembles as I cradle her to my chest. Her body's shaking, and ragged gasps escape her lips. My instinct is to protect her from whatever demons are chasing her. I tighten my arms around her while whispering soothing words into her ear. I've seen enough PTSD in my time in the service to understand what's going on here.

There's unhealed trauma in this woman's past, and something triggered it tonight.

The trembling eases as I carry her out of the woods. She nuzzles her head into me, her hair tickling the top of my neck and my throat.

She smells like floral shampoo and I breathe in deeply, loving the feminine scent of her.

As we come out of the woods into the fading twilight, large drops of rain fall from the sky. She

13

seems to be alone, but I peer into the tent just in case, keeping her pressed to me as I bend down.

There's nobody in the tent and not much gear either. Just a woman's purse, which I grab, guessing that it's belongs to the beauty in my arms.

Her breathing slows as I stride with her over to my truck. But I can tell she's still shaken.

I don't know who she is or where she's come from, but my urge to protect her is overwhelming. She's not just any tourist. She's a woman lost in the wilderness, in need of help, and I'm the man that's going to help her.

I glance up at the sky as large raindrops hit my forehead. It's almost dark now, with the thick clouds smothering the mountain.

We make it to my truck, and I pull open the passenger door as heavy raindrops splatter the window. The woman climbs into the front seat, and I dump her purse in the footwell and grab a blanket from the back. Her hands are shaking from cold and shock, so I help her do up her seatbelt and then tuck the blanket around her, right up to her chin.

She looks adorable bundled up like that. Her wide brown eyes watch me with a cross between embarrassment and curiosity.

"I'm taking you to safety," I tell her.

But there's no time to say anything more if I don't want to get drenched.

I slam her car door shut and jog around to the other side, hauling myself in as the heavens open up.

I start up the engine, and we make our way down the trail with the windshield wipers going full tilt.

There's no time to drop her off in town, not that I would anyway. This woman is mine, and there's only one place I'm taking her.

Flash floods can happen in the mountains when it rains this much and this fast. The sooner we get off the road the better.

"I'm Symon. I'm a Park Ranger. We're evacuating tourists off the mountain."

"I'm Leonie." Her voice comes out as a squeak, and she coughs to clear her throat. "Leonie."

She says again, this time with conviction in her voice. I like that. Leonie may appear meek at this moment, coming down from a panic attack and bundled up in a rainstorm, but I can tell my girl's got grit.

"Where are you taking me?"

I should take her into town. I should take her down the mountain and to a safe, dry hotel with the other evacuees. But there's only one place I'm taking Leonie.

"Home."

4

# LEONIE

I've never seen it rain so hard in all my nineteen years on this earth. Sure, we get our fair share of rain in Charlotte, but this is mountain rain. Torrential, sudden, and heavy.

When I think about being in that tent only ten minutes ago, a shiver goes through me. If this stranger hadn't have come along, I'm not sure how I would have survived the night.

It's no use trying to talk over the sound of the rain hitting the roof, so we drive in silence as I surreptitiously regard my savior.

His sandy blonde hair is plastered to his face, and droplets of rain hang off the ends of his wet strands. I have a sudden urge to run my hands through his hair and shake the rain off it.

The top of his uniform is wet and it clings to his

shoulders, showing the outline of thick muscles underneath. I know how strong this chest is because I leaned against it.

The memory makes my core tighten and sends wet heat between my legs. I've known this man for ten minutes, but my body is reacting as if I've known him all my life. I never experienced heat like this when I was around Grant.

Symon says he's taking me home. I guess he means his home, and that's fine with me. I sense I'm safe with this man, even though he's a stranger. Even though I should be wary of people. But when he scooped me into his arms, a calmness descended on me.

The drive down the mountain is slow, and Symon concentrates on the dark road and the rain pelting us from all sides.

I try to keep my gaze inside the pickup, ignoring the darkness that surrounds us.

It's embarrassing enough that I had a panic attack in the woods. I don't want Symon to know what caused it.

His rough hands expertly maneuver the steering wheel, guiding us around potholes and slippery corners. I can tell that he's a capable man who's probably not afraid of anything. I don't want him to realize what a silly, silly girl I am. A silly girl who's afraid of the dark.

He pulls into a dirt road, the headlights picking up brown puddles forming in the potholes.

The pickup slows down and I peer out of the windshield, not wanting to look beyond the beams of light. As we pull up a sensor light comes on, illuminating the front porch of a log cabin. I breathe a sigh of relief. There's light and shelter and a big helpful mountain man. I shrug the blanket off and pick up my purse.

"You ready to run?" Symon asks.

"Yeah."

I'm not. The thought of running through the dark, driving rain makes me queasy, but I don't want to show him that. So long as I can keep the light in my sights, I'll feel safe.

"Let's go."

I push the door open at the same time as Symon and jump out of the pickup. The rain pummels my entire body, whipping at my face and driving me backwards.

I've never felt rain like this before. I'm soaked before I even take my first step. I run for the light, trying to ignore the darkness that surrounds us. And run straight into Symon for the second time today.

He catches me just before I topple over and steadies me.

"Whoa there."

His firm grip on my arm cuts through the cold and wet and sends a warm shiver dancing across my chest. We stare at each other under the front awning of the cabin as the rain cascades down around us. A sizzle of energy passes between us so shocking that it makes me jump.

Symon smiles, an affable grin that softens his eyes.

"Let's get you inside."

He unlocks the door and flips on the light switch. I hesitate in following him in because I'm soaking wet.

"I don't want to drip all over your floor."

Mom would kill me if I entered the apartment like this and ruined her carpets. But Symon just shakes his head.

"Don't worry about it. The floors will recover."

I follow him in and stand dripping on the wooden floor, not sure what to do with my soaking clothes.

Symon shrugs off his boots. Then he's peeling off his wet shirt and starting on his pants.

My mouth pops open at the sight of his muscular body, slick with water. Tattoos run over his arms and down his back in intricate patterns. He's facing away from me, and his back flexes as he pulls off his pants, making the muscles dance.

My core clinches tight, and sticky heat mingles with the wetness between my legs.

He turns around and I spin around too, embarrassed that I've been caught staring. A man's never had this effect on me before, and heat rises up my neck to blush on my cheeks.

Symon lets out a low, throaty chuckle.

"Didn't mean to scare you, Leonie. I'll just grab some towels."

He pads across the wooden floor, leaving wet footprints. My gaze lingers on his boxer-clad butt as it jiggles down the hallway.

I'm breathless for the second time today. But this time it's a nice breathless, the type that lifts you up and makes you feel like you could fly.

Symon comes back a few moments later wrapped in a towel and hands another one to me. His chest is bare, and I try not to stare at his pink nipples surrounded by rings of dark curly hair.

"I'm running a bath for you."

There's a bead of water hanging off the end of his left nipple, and I wonder how it would taste if I were to bend down and lick if off with my tongue.

"It looks like you could do with a soak in the tub while I get the fire going."

My gaze flicks to his face and my cheeks heat, embarrassed that I've been caught ogling him again. But the man is a god among men. Muscular and sturdy, yet he's gentle and kind, not at all like the boys I grew up with.

"Thank you," I say, remembering my manners. "But I don't want to impose."

Symon's mouth twitches into a smile, and his hand reaches toward me. I hold my breath as he takes a wet strand of hair between his fingers and tucks it behind my ear.

It's a simple gesture, but his touch sends heat skittering through my body.

"You're not imposing, Leonie. You're my guest. And I take good care of my guests."

There's heat in his gaze, and his pale green eyes darken. Thoughts of him 'taking good care' of me make my mind skittish and do nothing to help the growing ache in my pussy.

He turns away to tend to the fire and I'm left dripping on the wooden floor, wondering what the heck this energy is between us.

I grab the towel and run it through my hair, shaking the water out of it. But I'm not about to remove my clothes the way Symon did. I'm a curvy girl. Short and round. There's no way I'm going to drop my clothes in front of this Adonis of a man.

I pad down the hall, leaving a wet trail as I go. It's easy to find the bathroom. There are only two doors down here. One I guess is Symon's bedroom, and the other is open with steam billowing out.

The bath is one of those old-fashioned tubs with brass claw feet. It looks out over the open window. I imagine during the day there's a beautiful view of the mountain. But all I see is darkness.

A shudder goes through me.

"I'll shut the blinds."

I hadn't realized Symon had followed me to the bathroom. He pulls the blinds closed, shutting out the darkness.

There are candles around the edge of the bath, and the orange glow is enough to make me feel warm and secure.

"You relax while I fix us something to eat."

"Thank you." I barely get the words out because I'm overcome with emotion. I don't even know this man, and he's showing me more kindness than my so-called friends.

Symon shuts the door behind him, and I peel my clothes off and sink into the water, letting out a sigh of satisfaction as my body relaxes and warmth engulfs me.

The shock of the afternoon turns to anger. I can't believe Grant left me all alone with the storm coming. I slide under the water, submerging myself in its warmth. When I resurface, all thoughts of Grant are gone. Because now there's another man taking up my mind. A strong, kind mountain man.

As the water eases my shock from the day and warms up my cold bones, I let my mind wander to Symon's rippling muscles when he pulled his shirt off. I imagine what it would be like to run my hands down his taut body. To feel him bulge and tremble underneath me. My pussy has been aching ever since he stripped drown in front of me and I slide my hand under the water and between my legs, imagining it's one of Symon's capable hands.

Just then, there's a knock at the door.

"Dinner's ready."

I jerk my hand out from between my legs, causing water to slosh over the sides of the tub.

"Be there in a minute!"

With thoughts of Symon dancing through my mind, I drain the water and dry myself.

Symon laid some of his own clothes out, and I slip into an oversized checkered shirt, loving the way it feels on me. A sigh escapes my lips as I catch his scent on the shirt.

It's a pleasant fantasy to have but, he won't want an inexperienced, short, stubby girl like me.

## 5
## SYMON

The sound of footsteps padding down the hall lets me know Leonie's out of the tub.

The protective feeling I've had since I saw her in a crumpled heap on the forest floor has only grown stronger since I got her back to my cabin. I want to look after her, to protect her from whatever demons she carries.

But until she opens up to me, I'll start with the practical stuff. A hot bath and a good meal.

I place two steaming bowls of pasta with thick tomato sauce down on the table.

"You want parmesan cheese on yours?"

The words die in my throat as Leonie walks around the corner. She's wearing the checkered shirt I laid out for her, and it comes to just above her bare knees. As she tilts her head to drag the towel through her wet hair the shirt rides up her legs, showing off thick, pale thighs.

My throat goes dry at the sight of her.

It's been far too long since I saw a woman's thighs, and I've never seen any as delicious as these. Her skin is flushed pink from the bath, and there's a dimple above the left knee.

"Yes please."

I tear my gaze away from her legs, but my eyes snag on her breasts pushed up against the buttons of my shirt. They're jiggling as she shakes out her hair, and the realization that she's not wearing a bra under the shirt has my cock as hard as the parmesan shaker I'm holding in my hand.

I take a long moment to remember the question that I asked her.

"Parmesan, right."

With a monumental effort, I shake some parmesan onto her pasta and take a seat at the table, all the while attempting to hide the aching bulge in my sweatpants. Leonie doesn't seem to notice or she's too shy to say. I'm just happy she's not running into the storm in fright.

We sit down to eat, and I take the time to study her closer.

Her skin is soft and unblemished. She looks innocent, but there's a defiance in her I like. I'm itching to know what she was doing alone in the storm, but something tells me to tread carefully.

"How old are you, Leonie?"

"I just turned nineteen."

Her eyes meet mine, challenging me to say something about her youth. She's fifteen years younger than me. The thoughts I'm thinking about her are indecent. Yet I know without a doubt that she's mine, and I'm not giving her up.

"Where are you from, because I guess that it's not around here?"

"Is it that obvious," she says with a smile. "I'm from Charlotte."

Charlotte's the biggest city in North Carolina. It's where a lot of our tourist come from.

"You like living in the city?"

She shrugs. "I guess. That's where I grew up, and I don't know any different."

The way she scrunches up her face tells a different story. This is a city girl who doesn't like her city. I'd bet on it.

She twirls pasta on her fork, playing with her food. "I guess I'd like to get away from my neighborhood, if I could."

I wonder if her reason for wanting to get away has anything to do with why she was freaking out in a tent in a storm.

If she's not tied to the city, that gives me hope. A vision of Leonie here on the mountain dances in my mind.

"Mountain life is good," I say, testing the waters.

"You know anyone who's hiring?"

She smiles, making a joke, but hell. I'll find a job for her just to keep her around.

My old army buddy Dylon is looking for a new nanny. He's a single dad and needs all the help he can get. The problem is that he's a grumpy bastard, and every nanny he hires quits.

It's on the tip of my tongue to tell her about the job, but something stops me.

I want to keep Leonie to myself. I don't want Dylon or any other man laying their eyes on her. The thought of Leonie living in Dylon's house and raising his kid makes me shudder.

"I'll ask around," I say.

We talk for a while. She asks about me and my background, and I ask more about her. I find out she lives with her mother and doesn't mention her father.

It's not until our bowls are empty and we've had seconds that I broach the subject I really want to ask.

"What were you doing up here camping on your own?"

She flinches at the question and looks down at the table. When she answers, her voice is quiet.

"I got left behind."

I stare at her, trying to figure out the circumstances of how that could happen.

"What do you mean, little one? How did you get left behind?"

"I came up here with a guy. We set up the tent, he said he was going out for a pee, and never came back."

Jealousy surges through my veins and I clench my fists, struggling to keep my tone light.

"You sure he's not still up there?"

She shakes her head. "No, he took the car."

Leonie's voice is a whisper, and she keeps her eyes downcast. The confident, smiling woman I've been talking to has disappeared. This is a diminished version of Leonie, a version who's been beaten down and made to feel like she's worthless. My fists clench at whoever did this to her, whoever put her light out.

With halting breaths, she tells me about Grant. How she fell for his lines, and how he made her feel special only to ditch her on the mountain as some kind of sick joke.

By the time she's finished telling the story, I'm pacing the kitchen with thoughts of everything I'll do to Grant once I find him racing through my mind.

How could anyone do that to a human being, let alone to Leonie? The sweetest, kindest, funniest woman I've ever met.

"When I find that asshole, I'll make him pay for what he did to you, Leonie."

She swipes a tear away with the back of her hand.

"Don't worry," she says hastily. "I don't want anyone getting hurt."

My anger is scaring her, and I make myself take deep breaths. I can deal with Grant later, but right now it's Leonie I need to focus on.

I kneel next to her and pull her chair around so that she's facing me.

"I'm sorry that happened to you, Leonie, but I'm glad that I found you."

I slide my finger under her chin and tilt her head up so she's looking at me.

"I'll take care of you now, okay?"

She nods slowly, her wide eyes looking at me hopefully. My urge to protect her is overwhelming. To make sure she's never abandoned like that again.

I pull her close to me, wrapping my arms around her protectively. Her body molds to mine, and she leans her head on my shoulder.

"I'll never leave you alone. You're safe here. You're safe with me."

A little sigh escapes her lips and I hold her tighter, until all the tension drains from her body and she feels the weight of my words. Because I mean them. I'm never letting her go.

A gust of wind rattles the windows and howls down the chimney. Reluctantly, I pull away from Leonie to add fresh logs to the fire.

After we clear up the dishes, I grab a tub of ice cream and two spoons. We settle on the couch in front of the fire. Leonie tucks her legs up under her, and I pull them out and stretch them across my lap.

She smiles at me shyly as I massage her small feet. We talk some more, and I don't mention the incident today.

I barely know this woman, but seeing her in my space and in my clothes causes a yearning in me that goes beyond the ache in my cock. It feels right for her to be here with me, where she belongs.

6

# LEONIE

$\mathcal{R}$ain batters the roof of the cabin, and the wind howls outside. But I hardly notice the storm. I'm snuggled up with Symon on the couch with a roaring fire before us. The way my body molds to his is the most natural thing in the world.

After the awkward conversation at dinner when I admitted, to my shame, that I was abandoned here on the mountain as a practical joke, Symon hasn't brought it up again, which I'm thankful for.

We talk easily despite the age difference. Symon's the first man who seems to get me, who can see beyond my looks.

My mother thought she was doing a good thing by sending me to a fancy school with the inheritance she got from my father. She didn't realize how cruel and entitled some of those kids could be. And how that cruelty followed me even after graduation.

But Symon's not like the boys I went to school with. He's more mature. A grown man who knows to look beyond my body's shape to see me for the person I am.

We talk until Symon puts the last log on the fire, laughing easily as we get to know each other.

I can't tell him yet about what caused the panic attack in the woods. I'm not ready to divulge my fear of the dark or how that came about, and he doesn't ask.

Instead, I tell him about where I grew up, the apartment I live in with my mom.

The restlessness I feel living in Charlotte. The yearning I have for something different but not knowing what that is. The discontent as I walk down the streets, feeling that I'm out of place, that I don't belong in this beautiful city with its beautiful people.

Symon tells me about his military service. He talks about his unit in the Special Forces and how many of them came to live here on Wild Heart Mountain.

My heart opens to this selfless man, who served his country and now serves his community as the

Mountain Ranger and a volunteer firefighter for Wild Heart Mountain.

He talks about that team as well and the busyness of the summer season.

I don't know what time it is when he shows me to the bedroom. There's only one bed and he's giving it up for me, another selfless act. But as he tucks the blankets around my chin and gives me a chaste kiss on the forehead, a pang of longing tugs at my core. I wish he would climb into the blankets with me and ease the ache that I've felt between my legs ever since he rescued me in the woods.

But I don't know how to ask. So I say goodnight as the door closes, leaving me alone with the wind howling outside and the rain pounding on the roof.

Yet, I feel safe here.

The bedside light gives a soft orange glow, and it's enough to banish the shadows. I'll keep it on all night as I always do.

It's comforting knowing that Symon is sleeping on the couch just down the hall. With thoughts of him on my mind, I drift off to sleep.


I awake with a start. It's pitch black, and my room is unfamiliar. The bed is too soft, the scent too woodsy.

My pulse picks up a notch as I fumble for the lamp, remembering where I am.

I find the lamp and flip the switch.

Nothing happens. I switch it back. Nothing again.

Swallowing down the panic, I lurch out of bed and stumble toward the light switch by the door. My arms are outstretched, and I bump into the wall and find the light switch.

But nothing happens when I flick it on. There must be a power outage from the storm.

The darkness closes in on me, and memories of that night flash through my mind. My heart races, and my breathing gets shallow.

Oh, no, no, no, no, no. Not here. Not now. Flinging open the door, I stumble down the hallway to Symon and safety before the panic can take hold.

Embers glow fiery red in the grate. It's enough light to illuminate Symon sleeping on the rug by the fire.

His sturdy form is a beacon of calmness through the rising storm of my panic. My breathing slows as I go to him. I crawl under the blanket and lie next to him, the warmth of his body calming my mind.

Without a word, he opens his arms and accepts me into them.

"There's been a power outage," I say, needing to

give him an explanation so he doesn't think I'm a foolish girl for being scared of the dark.

"Go to sleep, little one."

I bury my face in his chest, breathing in his woodsy sent. His hand runs over the back of my head, smoothing my hair in calming strokes.

My breathing steadies and my pulse slows. The panic subsides and is replaced by a quietness as he lulls me to sleep.

7

# SYMON

floral scent fills my nostrils, and heavy from sleep I breathe it in. There's a warm body pressed against me, feminine softness nestled into the crook of my arm.

My eyes flick open to find Leonie nuzzled into me with her mouth slightly open as she sleeps. Her hair falls over her forehead, and I resist the urge to move it for fear of waking her.

We stayed up talking late into the night. The connection between us is undeniable. It's a physical attraction, but it goes deeper than that. I know in my heart that Leonie is the woman for me. I've known it since I carried her out of the woods.

It was inevitable that she ended up in my arms last night. I watch her for a few moments until she stirs, a smile lighting up her face when she catches me looking at her.

"Good morning, beautiful."

Her smile gets even more radiant, making her natural beauty shine through. Then she realizes where she is and she sits up on her elbows, looking embarrassed.

"The power went off last night. Sorry."

She pulls back the blankets as if to get up, and I pull her toward me.

"It's okay, little one. I'll keep you safe."

She bites her lower lip and settles back against me.

She doesn't know that I want her to be here. That I'll take care of her and protect her from whatever demons had her running into my arms. She's mine to protect.

Leonie gives an enormous yawn, stretching her body. As she moves against me, a new urge fills my body. An urge to make her mine. To claim her as my woman.

Her arms go over her head, making her tits push outwards, and I use the opportunity to roll on top of her, pinning her underneath me.

She gives a startled yelp, her mouth popping open in an adorable 'o.'

"You look beautiful in the morning."

Her lips pull into a smile, and her pupils dilate.

"So do you."

I chuckle, because no one's ever called me beautiful before, but fuck me. With this woman underneath me, my very soul's glowing.

She parts her lips expectantly, and I press my mouth to hers. The kiss is soft and gentle, full of the sweetness and innocence that is Leonie.

I love the way she lights me up. Like no woman has before.

I roll her against me so we're lying side by side. My hand clasps her face as I kiss her gently. Wanting to make up for every hurt and everything that's ever scared her, wanting to show her the goodness and gentleness that she deserves.

As I'm being gentle, Leonie wiggles her body against mine, grinding her hips against my aching cock.

She may be all innocent and light, but her hips are telling me a different story, that there's a wildness inside her that wants to come out.

My arm wraps around her waist, and I move my hand down to the soft curve of her buttocks. She gasps as I pull her against me, and her eyes widen as my hard length sinks into her soft belly.

"I've been wanting to kiss you ever since you ran straight into me yesterday."

She gives an embarrassed giggle. "I thought you were a bear."

Her small hands slide under my t-shirt and run over my chest. She pushes the fabric up, and her mouth encloses my nipple.

I groan at the unexpected move, at her boldness, and her hot, wet mouth on me.

"And I've been wanting to do that ever since you stripped down in front of me."

Her teeth skim my nipple, causing sparks of heat to jolt through my body. My already aching cock twitches against her, and I roll my hips until it nestles between her legs.

"Be careful." My lips skim the top of her silky head. "If you touch me like that, there will be consequences."

She gives me a wicked grin and moves to my other nipple. Christ, she's got a slutty side that I can't wait to explore.

But I want to be the one making her writhe as I suck on her nipples.

Pulling her head up, I slide down so I can capture her lips in mine and kiss her hard.

She's still wearing my top, and I slide a hand up underneath to cup her heavy breasts. My palm runs over her nipple and then I clasp it in my fingers, making her gasp. Her head tilts back and my tongue runs up her neck until I get to her mouth.

This time when we kiss it's full of heat, full of passion, full of all the things we want to do to each other.

It takes a while to realize there's someone knocking on the front door.

Our kiss breaks apart and we stare at each other, panting.

The knock comes again, an insistent banging.

"Fuck."

The downside of staying in the Rangers Cabin in the park is that you're always on duty.

Leonie's breathing hard under me. Her top has fallen open, revealing one white globe heaving up and down.

Her lips are swollen and parted, and her eyes are wide. I'm so ready to claim this woman, and she's ready to be claimed. Ready for me to drive my hard cock into her.

The knocking comes again, and I can't ignore it. With the storm we had last night, someone could be in trouble. I'm the Mountain Ranger, and I have a duty to my community.

"I need to get this, little one." I plant a kiss right on her pink nipple, and I can't resist flicking my tongue out. "Wait right here. I'll be back."

As I walk to the door I adjust my sweatpants, trying to hide the dripping hard-on.

"This better be fucking good."

I pull open the door, and there's an athletic kid with his fist raised to knock.

"Whaddaya want?"

The kid's eyes widen when he sees me, but I'm not bothering to hide my scowl. This better be good or he's going to get it.

He's a city kid. In jeans that hang too low on his hips and a college sweatshirt.

"Uh - are you the Ranger?"

"Yeah."

I'm usually more personable but not today. He stares at me, swallowing hard and waiting for me to say something.

"There's a woman missing."

His words snap me out of my foul mood. I'm here to serve the community, and if someone's missing on the mountain then they need my help.

"Where did you last see her?"

The kid runs a hand through his hair. "We were camping at Lonely Ridge campsite."

It's the campsite where I found Leonie. This can't be a coincidence.

"She went missing during the storm. I woke up in the night, and she was gone."

My fists clench at the audacity of the lie. This asshole can't even own up to the fact that he left Leonie on her own.

Rage floods my veins, and I grab the top of his sweatshirt. The kid's eyes bulge in fright and surprise.

"You left a woman alone on a mountain during a storm."

"I-I-I didn't mean to. I was coming back."

There are footsteps behind me, and relief floods his face.

"Leonie. Thank God you're all right. I was worried."

This guy doesn't know what worried is. He was probably worried that he was going to get into trouble when he turned up this morning and found the tent wrecked and Leonie gone.

"You don't leave anyone on the mountain." I shake him as I say it so his teeth rattle, and terror returns to his eyes.

"It-it was a joke. Wasn't it, Leonie?"

I look back at Leonie, and she's turned white.

"I don't see her laughing."

He shuffles his feet, trying to get out of my grasp as I pull my arm back, ready to pummel his lying face.

"Symon."

Leonie's hand on my shoulder makes me pause. But only for a moment. I don't care if she's forgiven him. I'm not letting him off.

But when I glance at Leonie, it's not forgiveness in her expression. She's got a steely determination in her eyes as she narrows them at Grant.

"Let me."

She pulls her arm back, her hand forming a perfect fist. Grant's eyes go wide in shock as Leonie's fist connects with his face. He howls in pain as blood pours out of his nose.

Leonie shakes out her hand, wincing but looking satisfied.

She's full of surprises and definitely not the meek, innocent woman she first appeared to be. My girl's got spirit, and I fall in love with her a little bit more.

The fact that she can stand up for herself sends a shot of lust through my veins. I have to have her now.

I let go of Grant with a shove, sending him falling backwards down the porch steps.

"Leonie's with me now. She's mine, you understand."

He nods then winces as pain shoots up his broken nose.

"Now get the fuck off my mountain."

The kid turns and flees, and I watch until he's gotten in his pimped up car and reversed down my driveway.

When I turn back to Leonie, she's trembling.

Our eyes meet, and there's no need for words. Our needs are more carnal than that.

I scoop her off her feet and into my arms, carrying her into the bedroom.

"You're mine, Leonie. And I'm going to claim you."

She pouts her lips in the most adorable way that makes my cock rock hard. She's innocent, this woman. I'm pretty sure she's a virgin, and I can't wait to claim what's mine.

I lay her down on the bed and slowly peel her clothes off as I kiss every part of her body. I mean to go slow and gentle, but the way she writhes under me makes it impossible.

My hand slides down to her pussy folds, and they're wet and glistening.

"You're wet for me, baby."

She moans, capturing my hand in hers and pressing it between her legs.

"I want you to touch me. I want you to touch my pussy."

The dirty words coming from her innocent mouth take me by surprise. She's full of surprises, and every single one of them makes me harder for her.

"Put your finger in my tight cunt."

I groan at her dirty mouth as my finger slides into her.

She gasps, and her hips buck as a soft moan escapes her lips.

"Is this your first time, little one?"

"Yes, Symon." Her wide eyes find mine. "I want it to be with you. I want you to fuck me. To take my virginity and claim my pussy."

Dirty words shouldn't be allowed on a mouth sweet as hers. I kiss her hard, moving my lips to her throat, wanting to hear her keep talking.

"I want you so much, Symon. I want you to put your cock in me."

She whines, so needy, so dirty. Her legs open up, her body transformed. The innocent girl is gone, and in front of me is the dirty slut she keeps hidden inside.

I'm aching to give her my cock, but she's so tight. If I go in without warming her up it will hurt her, and that's the last thing I want to do.

"Be patient. I wanna make you come first. Then I'll give you my cock. I promise."

As I say the words, I slide another finger inside her. She moans, her face contorting in pleasure and surprise. Her hips move so she's bearing down on my palm.

"It feels so good." Her voice is breathy and needy and has my cock dripping precum.

With her back arched and tits in the air, she takes one hand and moves her fingers around her breast, tweaking her own nipples.

It's the most erotic sight I've ever seen, and if I keep watching I'll explode in my pants.

I dip my head between her legs and nuzzle into her thighs, planting kisses on her soft skin as I move up to her drenched core.

When my mouth closes over her pussy, she whimpers my name. I lick up all her feminine juices as I pump my fingers into her tight cunt.

Her hands grab my hair and she pulls my mouth against her, rubbing her clit up and down my tongue like a dirty, needy slut.

I love how she whimpers my name as she pushes herself into my face. How she comes alive under my touch.

My fingers pump her harder and harder as my tongue skates over her clit.

"Yeah, like that," the dirty slut whimpers. "Just there. Yeah, like that. Fuck me with your fingers." I pump her harder as she tightens around me.

"Fuck me. Fuck me, fuck me!" she screams as she comes undone on my tongue.

She cries out my name as her hands grip my hair and her legs stick straight into the air.

Only when she stops shaking does she let go of my head. I slide up the bed and kiss her mouth and she kisses me hungrily, taking in her pussy juices and licking her lips when I pull away.

"Can you fuck me now?" Her eyes are pleading and her legs are already wrapping around my hips, her fingers grabbing my ass and pulling me towards her.

She's dripping wet, and her cunt on the tip of my cock is too juicy and inviting. I don't want anything to be between us.

"I'm clean, Leonie."

She wiggles impatiently, but I make her pause to understand what I'm saying. "Is there any reason I shouldn't fuck you bare?"

"I'm a virgin, Symon, but I'm not on birth control."

The thought of Leonie's belly swollen with my baby is almost enough to make me come undone.

"Good. I want to breed you. I want you to have my baby."

Her eyes widen. "I want that too."

My tip circles her glistening opening, and she whimpers with need.

"I'm going to breed you so you're stuck here with me on the mountain. I'll make you my wife. Do you want that?"

"Yes." She nods. "I want all of it, Symon. I want it now."

I thrust into her, my dick ramrod hard at the thought of Leonie thick with my child. She screams as I shatter her virgin barrier and I hold her in place as she bucks her hips, waiting for the pain to ease.

"That's it, little one. It'll feel good now."

Her eyes are wide and wild, and her nostrils flare. I pull out as her virgin blood trickles out of her pussy and onto her thighs.

The sight sends me into a frenzy, and I thrust again.

This time she pushes her hips forward to meet me, her legs wrapping around my waist and her nails digging into my back.

"That's it. Take it like a good little slut."

She moans at the dirty talk, and with every thrust she chants my name.

"I've been waiting for your cock, Symon. I've been waiting for your big cock."

The dirty talk gets her off as much as it does me. My balls pull up tight, and I don't think I can last any longer. Then she's gripping me with her pussy as it convulses with her release.

I let myself go, exploding inside of her, shattering apart and sending my cum deep into her womb, hoping that it finds its mark.

As the seeds of my semen settle inside her, I plant soft kisses on her forehead. I stay in her as she nestles into my arms, knowing that I want this girl tied to me forever. She's exhausted, and with my cock still inside her, she dozes off to sleep.

8

LEONIE

A day spent with Symon is the happiest I've been for as long as I can remember.

Symon takes me out in his pickup with him. There's debris to be cleared after the storm and I step in and help the other volunteers.

We check in at the Lonely Ridge camping spot and grab Grant's tent, which is still standing.

The conversation flows throughout the day, and we laugh and chat together. I feel like I belong here on this mountain. Like there's a place for me here with Symon.

It's only when evening falls that I become uneasy. It's with relief that we head back to the cabin before sunset.

I haven't told him yet about that part of my past and about the fear I have of the dark. I've had the perfect day, and I don't want him to think any less of me. I don't want to let him down.

We're just finishing up the washing up when Symon takes my hand.

"I want to show you something."

He leads me towards the door and opens it into the dark night. I hesitate, but Symon picks up a lantern.

"I know you don't like the dark, Leonie, so I'll bring the light. But I want to show you something among the darkness that might help."

I shouldn't be surprised that he's noticed my fear of the dark. I don't want to go into the darkness, but I trust him. Maybe it's time to face my fear.

With a deep breath for courage, I let him lead me outside.

He holds the lantern up and I focus on the light, keeping my line of sight on the orange streak it provides on the ground ahead of us.

He leads me a little away from the house, then lays out a picnic blanket on the grass. We sit down and I keep my eyes on the lantern and my hand in Symon's, trying to ignore the dark surrounding us.

He pulls me down onto the blanket, and we lie side by side on our backs. Panic grips my chest and I roll onto my side, burrowing my face into Symon's side with my eyes closed.

"Look up."

Symon gently rolls my body away so that I'm on my back. With my hand squeezing Symon's, I dare to open my eyes.

I gasp at the sight laid out before me. Millions of stars twinkle in the black sky, tiny pinpricks of hope.

Symon squeezes my hand. "There can be beauty in darkness."

The whole of the Milky Way is spread out above us, and I've never seen such a wondrous sight.

"It's beautiful."

"You're beautiful."

Symon pulls me close to him, his warm breath tickling my ear.

"Do you think you could get used to this place?"

My heart skips a beat. I love it out here during the day, but at night... It's time to come clean to Symon, to let him know about my fear, who I truly am.

"I'm scared of the dark." My voice sounds small and childish even to myself. "I know that's stupid and childish and irrational, but I can't help it."

He props himself up on one elbow and brings the lantern around so our faces are lit up.

"Tell me about it, Leonie. What happened to you?"

His finger strokes my cheek, giving me the reassurance I need to tell him my story.

I tell him about my father. About the night me and him were home alone while Mom was away for a work conference. About the noises that I heard and how I went to get Dad. He told me to wait on the stairs while he went to investigate.

There'd been a power outage and it was dark, but that didn't bother me then. I waited in the dark, my ears straining to hear.

There were noises in the kitchen, a man shouted, and there was a scuffle. The sounds of a man groaning. I ran toward the noise, calling out for Dad.

A window smashed, and someone ran out into the street. I found Dad's flashlight on the floor, and when I flicked it on there was blood all over the tiles.

It was too late to save him. He disturbed a burglar and paid the ultimate price. And I had sat there in the dark listening to him die.

Symon lets me talk, listening to my story with patience and concern.

"It sounds like you have PTSD."

I frown at him. "Isn't that something that soldiers get?"

"Yeah. That's how I recognize it. But anyone who's experienced trauma can suffer from it. Did you ever have counselling or anything like that?"

"No, Mom was devastated. She blamed herself for not being there. I felt like I had to look after her."

I was nine years old when it happened. Old enough to put on a brave face and not let anyone see how I was reliving the incident every night when the lights went out. If I left the lights on, the dreams didn't bother me. It was a way to cope, but over the years it developed into a fear of the dark, of what might hide in the shadows.

"You can let that responsibility go. I'll take care of you now, and we'll get help for your mom if she needs it."

His fingers cup my cheek, and I lean into his touch. No one's looked after me like this for a long time.

I close my eyes, drawing strength from his words as they sink into my soul.

"Keep your eyes closed, Leonie, and know that I'm here."

I hear a click as the lantern goes off. My pulse quickens, but then Symon's lips are on mine, kissing me slowly.

I peek my eyes open and the stars twinkle down from above, casting him in a halo of light. My gaze shifts to the darkness around us, and my body stiffens. Symon runs his hand down my side.

"I'm here. I'm keeping you safe. Close your eyes and let me take care of you."

With my heart racing, I do as he says.

I'm not sure if it's the terror or the excitement of his touch, but my blood is thundering in my ears as his hands move over my body. I give in to the sensation as he unbuttons my top and slides his rough hands over my soft breasts.

Not being able to see him intensifies every sensation. His rough skin on mine, the tickle of his breath as he kisses my throat, his scent of pines and woodsmoke, and the taste of his lips sweet from the apple pie we had with dinner.

His hands tug at my panties, and he pulls them off. The chilly night air on my pussy sends shivers skittering up my spine. I arch my back as my core clenches.

A needy heat simmers though my body. My fear dissipates, giving in to stronger sensations.

"I've got you, Leonie," Symon whispers in my ear. "You're safe with me."

He whispers calming words as his hands strum my body, his palms moving expertly between my legs. I moan into the night, enjoying every heightened sensation that it brings.

By the time his cock is circling my entrance, I'm dripping with need.

He slides into me slowly, so I experience every hard ridge of his shaft. I've never felt so full and so needy all at once.

This morning was fast and urgent, but this is slow and calm. This is something deeper. The connection between us coming out in the way our bodies mold to each other.

I open my eyes, finding Symon's soft gaze in the darkness. Around us is the night but I focus on Symon, listening to his words, the breeze tickling my skin as his cock fills me up.

He slowly moves in and out of me, my hips rolling with his, pushing me further up the peak until I fall over the edge, coming undone around him. I'm climbing a wave of sensation, and I soar up and up and up into the sky.

My spirit has left my body, and I'm looking down on us. And then I flutter down to earth, panting hard.

Before I have time to catch my breath, Symon picks up my body and flips me over. There's a new roughness to his touch as he pulls my hips up so I'm on all fours.

My gaze rests on the blanket as he rams into me from behind. There's nothing tender about the way Symon fucks me, taking what he needs from my body.

He grabs my tits as he pulls me to him, jackhammering into me like a rabbit. It's so hard and so dirty and so indecent, and his fingers move between my legs until I'm crying out again, screaming his name into the night.

That's when he releases into me. He shoots deep inside, hitting the back of my womb with his seed. I offer up a silent prayer that this one finds it mark, that I can have this man's babies.

It's not until we lie together afterwards, looking up at the stars, that I realize the lantern is still off. The only light is the stars above. But I'm calm. Calm and content in a way that I haven't been for many years.

Symon props himself up on one elbow to look down at me, his finger lazily tracing the curvature of my breast.

"Stay with me, Leonie."

We barely know each other, and even though it feels so right, there's something nagging at me.

"Are you serious? It's not a joke."

His eyes darken. "I've never been more serious in my life. Come live with me on the mountain and be my mountain girl."

I don't even have to think about it. My heart knows that this is right, that this is the man for me. He makes me feel safe. He protects me like no one else can, and for that I'll follow him to the ends of the earth.

"Yes," I say. "I'll stay. But you're gonna need a bigger cabin."

His eyes twinkle, and he rolls onto me again.

"I'll build you one just as soon as I get a baby in your belly."

He's hard already, and I'm ready to take him. This time it's a quick ride, sealing the deal of our future. He'll be my family forever, right here on the mountain.

Grant left me here as a practical joke, but I got the last laugh. I've got my military mountain man, a genuine hero, and I couldn't be happier.

# EPILOGUE

## LEONIE

Five years later...

The light of the fire casts an orange hue over the faces of Symon and our two oldest kids. They spear thick marshmallows onto the ends of sticks, and Symon shows them the perfect way to rotate the sticks in the embers.

Trinity's stick drops into the fire, and when she lifts it up the marshmallow is grey with ash. She lets out a howl of disappointment and Symon scoops her into his arms, ready with a new marshmallow to shove into her chubby fingers.

She's a real daddy's girl that one. At three years old, she's already got her father wrapped around her little finger.

On the other side of the fire, Kobe's kids are

getting the same help from their dad. They're a little too young to do it themselves, but they'll learn.

"You gotta hold it out of the flames, sweetheart," calls Hailey from the sidelines.

She's keeping me company as I feed the baby. We're sitting back toward the house, keeping away from the smoke of the fire.

It's a warm autumn night, and I've got the little one wrapped up in a blanket as she feeds from my breast.

It's been six years since I found Symon on the side of the mountain, or he found me, I should say. Six years of pure happiness.

I was pregnant a few months after we met, and we haven't stopped breeding since.

When the ranger's cabin got too small for us, we moved further up the mountain into a bigger cabin to accommodate our expanding family.

Symon taught me all about the mountain, and I've grown to love it. I work part-time at the visitor's center, but I've had so much time off with the babies, I'm not sure I want to go back.

"They're only young once," I say to Hailey for the hundredth time.

We've been having this conversation back and forth for the last few years. Both of us are torn between wanting to spend time with our children and wanting to do something for ourselves.

Hailey founded the woman's refuge center with her sister, Trish. But if I'm honest with myself, I've never been one to hunger after a career. I'm happy being taken care of by Symon while raising our children. I'm busy enough keeping the cabin in order and wrangling the little ones.

With Symon's support, I got the counselling I needed and could put my childhood trauma behind me. I'll never forget Dad, but I'm not afraid of the dark anymore.

I convinced Mom to get proper help too. We created a memorial to Dad in one of his favorite city parks, and that helped Mom move on as well.

Trinity's giggle brings my attention back to the present. She's sitting next to her older brother on an overturned log munching on s'mores.

Symon looks up, and our eyes lock. His gaze softens as he takes in me feeding the baby, and a content smile spreads across his face.

He was my light that led me out of the darkness, my protector and my savior.

Five years ago, I was taken by a mountain man, but now I choose to stay. And that has made all the difference.

# CHOSEN BY THE MOUNTAIN MAN

**She's the nanny, half my age and off limits. But my heart has chosen her, even if it breaks me...**

My military career ended when I became a widower.

My daughter needed me, so I came back to Wild Heart Mountain determined to be a good father.

Except I'm not. I'm too grumpy, too bitter, too broken.

Until Caitlin walks through the door. She's all sunshine and smiles, shining her light into the dark corners of my heart.

The military broke me, but Caitlin has the power to utterly destroy me...or heal me.

My heart has chosen her, but will she choose me?

*Chosen by the Mountain Man* is a single dad and nanny, grumpy/sunshine, age gap romance featuring an ex-military flawed hero and the curvy, innocent woman his heart chooses. A short, sweet, and steamy instalove romance.

Dylon

"Ow, Dad, you're pulling too tight." Karmel's eyes scrunch up in the mirror as she gives me her best angry face. "And it doesn't look right."

I push pause on the YouTube video *"Easy princess hair for your little princess!!!"* But in the process of extracting myself, her hair tangles around my fingers and I yank on a strand.

"Owwww." She elongates the vowel as her eyes water.

"Sorry, sweetheart. I suck at this kind of thing."

I survey my work in the mirror.

It's nothing like the plaited configuration she wants. The bun leans to the left, strands of hair hang over her face where they shouldn't, and the plait is uneven.

She's trying out for the princess role in her school play and insisted we test out the style today before I have to do it next week before school.

Despite living halfway up a mountain where she can climb trees, trap animals, and run around in the dirt as much as she likes, my little girl still wants to be a princess. It's not uncommon to find her stomping around the property in her favorite pink tulle princess costume and rainboots.

Our eyes meet in the mirror, both the same dark brown. Hers are wincing, but from the pain I've caused or from the disaster that's sitting on top of her head, I'm not sure.

Karmel twists the stray strands into the bun, trying to make it less lopsided. "When are we getting a new nanny?"

I look away and tidy up the bobby pins that are spread over my dresser. When I left the military to look after my daughter, I knew I couldn't do it alone. We've been through a string of nannies over the last six years. But none of them stick around for long.

"I don't know, sweetie. Soon."

The agency sent me a new CV to look through, but I haven't opened it yet. Every time a new nanny starts and then leaves, it breaks Karmel's heart all over again.

"Why did you have to scare Jannie away?"

Jannie was the last nanny, a middle-aged woman who stayed for exactly two weeks until I caught her driving Karmel without a seatbelt on.

"I didn't scare her away. Jannie wasn't up to the job."

"It was only up the driveway, and she didn't know I'd taken it off."

Karmel's pouting at me, but we've been through this argument before. Karmel claims she took her own seatbelt off as soon as they turned into the driveway, because she wanted to get something out of her schoolbag in the back seat.

The driveway is a long gravel access road, and my cabin is the only place it leads to. There are potholes, and animals could run across at any moment. I was coming out of my workshop as they pulled up and saw Karmel in the front seat with no seatbelt on. Even thinking about it, what might have happened, makes me mad.

"It's the principle of the thing," I tell her for the hundredth time. "You don't take your belt off until the car comes to a stop and the engine is off."

"But it was my fault. Jannie didn't have to get fired for it."

She pouts at me, her lower lip wobbling at the perceived injustice. She thinks I was too harsh, but there's no such thing when it comes to my daughter.

"It's the driver's responsibility. Jannie should have insisted you keep your belt on." I swipe my hand in the air to emphasize my point, which only makes me sound harsher than I intended.

"But Jannie was nice." Tears spring from her eyes. "You always scare away the nannies with your stupid rules. No one will ever stay with us. I look like a witch not a princess, and it's all your fault!"

Karmel throws down the bobby pins and storms out of the bathroom. A few moments later, her bedroom door slams so hard the photo on my dresser wobbles and falls over.

I've done it again. I've upset my daughter. She doesn't understand that I'm hard on the nannies for her sake. Karmel's the most precious thing in my life, and I can't let anything happen to her like it did her mother.

I pick up the photo that toppled over. It's one of me and Michelle, on vacation in Florida one time I was back on leave and before Karmel was born. I'm clean shaven with a short military haircut and smiling bright eyes. One arm is draped casually around Michelle as we each hold a cocktail. Our smiles could light up a Christmas tree.

Loud sobs come from Karmel's bedroom, letting me know I'm not forgiven for chasing away the only nanny she liked this year.

"You were always better at this than me."

Michelle smiles back at me as if to say, 'You've got this.'

Even though I haven't.

"I can't let anything bad happen to her. You understand, right?"

I don't know if Michelle can hear me from wherever it is she went to. But her silence speaks volumes.

If she was here, we'd laugh about how difficult kids are. She'd go in and smooth things over, do Karmel's hair and sing to her until she's laughing again.

But Michelle's not here. So I have to navigate this on my own, the only way I know how.

I put the photo back in place and stand up. Karmel can cry all she wants, but I won't back down on any decision I make to keep her safe. I don't care if we go through a hundred nannies. I'm not letting my girl come to any harm.

To keep reading, visit:
https://mybook.to/WHMMilitaryHeroes

# GET YOUR FREE BOOKS

Sign up to the Sadie King mailing list and get access to all the bonus content including bonus scenes and five FREE steamy short romances!

You'll be the first to hear about new releases, exclusive offers, bonus content and all my news. You can even email me back. I love chatting with my readers!

To claim your free ebooks visit:

authorsadieking.com/bonus-scenes

If you're already a subscriber check your last email for the link that will take you straight to the bonus content.

BOOKS AND SERIES BY SADIE KING

**Wild Heart Mountain**

Military Heroes

Wild Riders MC

Mountain Heroes

Temptation

A Runaway Bride for Christmas

A Secret Baby for Christmas

Knocked Up

**Sunset Coast**

Underground Crows MC

Sunset Security

Men of the Sea

Love and Obsession (The Cod Cove Trilogy)

For a full list of titles check out the Sadie King website

www.authorsadieking.com

# ABOUT THE AUTHOR

Sadie King is a USA Today Best Selling Author of over 120 short and steamy contemporary romances. She loves writing about military heroes and the sassy women who heal their hearts.

Sadie lives in New Zealand with her ex-military husband and raucous young son.

When she's not writing she loves catching waves with her son, running along the beach, and drinking good wine, preferably with a book in hand.

Sign up to her newsletter to receive all the latest news and releases and access to exclusive bonus content.

www.authorsadieking.com

www.ingramcontent.com/pod-product-compliance
Lightning Source LLC
Chambersburg PA
CBHW031401160726

47993CB00003B/1066